# This That Little Pig

Characters

**Narrator**

**Pig 1**

**Pig 2**

**Pig 3**

**Pig 4**

**Pig 5**

Setting

The pigs' home and town

# Picture Words

food

read

# Sight Words

| eat | had | have | I |
|-----|-----|------|---|
| like | some | to | want |

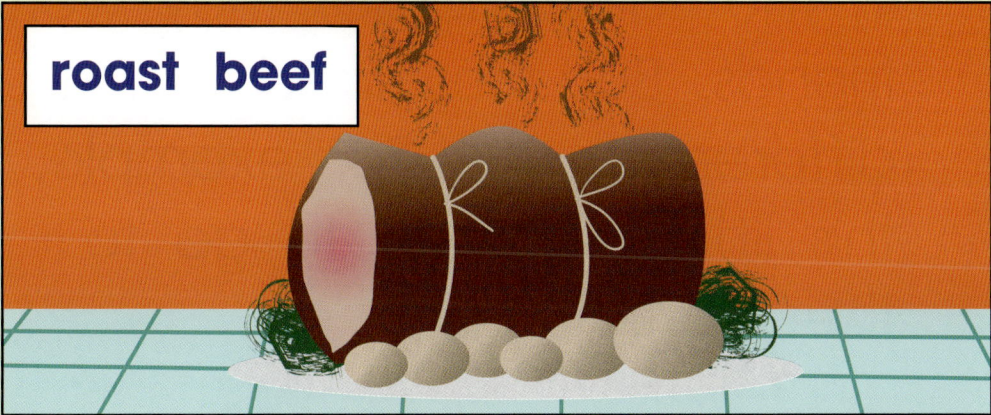

roast beef

shop

## Enrichment Words

home

market

stay

**Narrator:** Five little pigs lived in the same house. They were friends. But they liked to do different things. For example, this little pig liked to go to the market.

**Pig 1:** Shop, shop, shop. I like to shop.

**Pig 2:** I do not like to shop. I like to stay home.

**Pig 1:** Then stay home.

**Pig 2:** I will stay home. I like to read.

**Pig 1:** Have fun. Bye!

**Narrator:** This other little pig liked to eat.

**Pig 3:** Food, food, food. I like to eat.

**Narrator:** This pig liked roast beef best.

**Pig 3:** Roast beef! Yum, yum!

**Pig 4:** Hey! I want to eat, too. I want some roast beef.

**Pig 3:** All gone!

**Pig 4:** I had none! None! You are a pig!

**Pig 3:** I know . . .

**Narrator:** And that little pig—

**Pig 5:** La, la, la.

**Narrator:** That pig liked to play all day long.

**Pig 5:** I like to play. Wee, wee, wee!

La, la, la

**Narrator:** And he went "wee, wee, wee" all the way home.

**Pig 5:** Wee, wee, wee!

## The End